Curious George®
Windy Delivery

Adaptation by Adah Nuchi
Based on the TV series teleplay written by Ross Canter

Houghton Mifflin Harcourt
Boston New York

For information about permission to reproduce selections from this book, write to Permissions, Houghton Mifflin Harcourt Publishing Company, 215 Park Avenue South, New York, New York 10003.

ISBN: 978-0-544-32075-8 paper over board
ISBN: 978-0-544-32076-5 paperback

Design by Afsoon Razavi
www.hmhco.com
Printed in China
SCP 10 9 8 7 6 5 4 3 2 1
4500483431

George loved to help his friend Bill deliver newspapers on his bicycle. Bill never missed his target, and he never ever missed a delivery day. One more day would make a perfect year and earn Bill the town's Golden Pouch award.

But when George woke up the next morning, it was not a perfect day. It was very snowy! George wondered how Bill would ride his bike in so much snow.

George went to see his friend. Bill was pedaling and pedaling, but he wasn't going anywhere. He was stuck!

"Can you believe this, George?" Bill asked. "The biggest day of my career and I can't even get out of my driveway."

George wanted to help. He gave Bill's bike a push. That got Bill going . . . but then he couldn't stop! Bikes did not work well in the snow.

Luckily, their neighbor Allie had something that did.

"Do you want to borrow my sled?" she asked.

"I've never used a toboggan before," said Bill. "Thanks, Allie. Now we might be able to deliver all the newspapers on time."

George and Bill were off!

Everything was going well until George and Bill
had to veer around a curve. They did not know how to steer.
Crash! Their neighbor Mr. Quint came running over. "Are you boys all right?"
he cried.

Mr. Quint invited them inside to warm up with a blanket. "Do you kids know how to steer the sled?" Mr. Quint asked. "You just need to lean into the turn."

Back on the toboggan, George and Bill had no trouble steering this time.
When they got to the big curve, they leaned, and leaned, and went around
it perfectly.
Now they were making great time. There was only one paper left to deliver.

But then George and Bill came to a complete stop. They had run out of hill.

They tried pulling the toboggan, but pulling was hard. "We'll never make it at this rate," said Bill. The wind was so strong.
George wondered if they could use the wind to help them move.

"Great idea, George! We can turn this blanket into a sail!" said Bill. "Now all we need are a mast and a boom." Bill explained that those are the two poles used to hang sails. The mast goes up and down, and the boom goes sideways across the bottom.

A hole in the toboggan was the perfect place for a
mast. All George needed was a couple of poles. A recycling bin nearby
provided exactly what they needed: a broom and a dustpan on a pole.

George and Bill removed the bristles and dustpan so that they had two poles.
The handles clipped together with a snap.

George and Bill were ready to hang
the sail. They folded the blanket into
a triangle. Once it was sail shaped,
they needed to attach their sail to
the poles. Luckily there were a few hooks
in the recycling bin, and attaching the sail
to the mast and boom was a breeze.

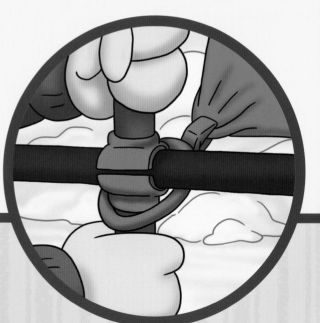

The sail was all set. They just needed something to help keep it in place. They put the dustpan back on the bottom. It held everything up and made the perfect newspaper holder, too!
George and Bill were ready to go!

But their sled wasn't going anywhere. "What if we turn the sail so it catches the wind?" asked Bill. He tied George's scarf to the boom so they could move the sail. The sail caught the wind and they were off! They only needed one more perfect delivery to get the Golden Pouch.

But it was 4:45 p.m. "We'll never make it all the way around the lake by five o'clock!" cried Bill. George knew they didn't have to go around the lake. It was frozen. They could go across it! It was another great idea.

In fact, it was such a great idea, Bill let George do the honors and deliver the last paper. George tossed it to the exact right spot.

Bill had earned his Golden Pouch.
"I couldn't have done it without you, partner," Bill said, "and I think you deserve to wear the pouch. Day one of a new delivery year starts tomorrow. Think we can win again?"

George was certain they would. When it came to paper delivery, it was always smooth sailing with Bill.

Let the wind blow!

George and Bill discovered that the wind could help their sled move.
What else can the wind move?

What you need:

- a plastic straw
- objects of various weights, such as a cotton ball, feather, small rock, plastic spoon, coin, paper cup, and wooden block
- a hard, flat surface such as a table or the floor

Predict which objects can be moved by the wind and which cannot.
Place the objects on a hard surface one at a time. Use your straw
to blow wind at the objects and try to make them move.
Were your predictions correct?

Set sail!

George and Bill learned that a sailboat has many parts. Here are some of the most common
parts of a sailboat:

HULL: The body, or bottom, of a sailboat.
SAIL: A piece of material that catches the wind and helps a boat move.
MAST: The vertical pole that the sail is attached to.
BOOM: A horizontal pole that attaches to the bottom of the sail.

Can you help George and Bill make sure their sailboat is complete
by pointing to each of the parts of this sailboat?

Special delivery!

When George and Bill delivered newspapers, they discovered that bikes do not work well in snow. But some things do! Can you help George and Bill make a perfect delivery by guessing which is the best mode of transportation for each terrain?

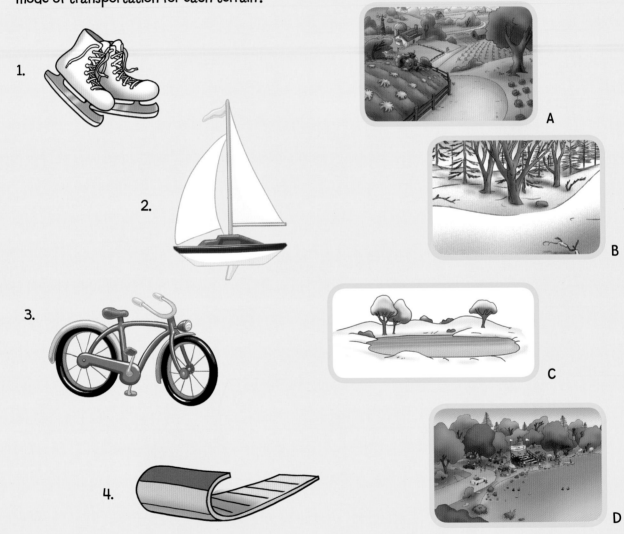

1.

2.

3.

4.

A

B

C

D